EMILY and SAM

The Case of the Missing Turtle

A Math Adventure

EMILY and SAM

The Case of the Missing Turtle

A Math Adventure

Book 1

in the **EMILY** and **SAM** Series

by

Dave Cole

Common Deer Press

Published by Common Deer Press Incorporated

Published in 2024 by Common Deer Press
1745 Rockland Avenue
Victoria, British Columbia
V8S 1W6

This book is a work of fiction. Names, characters,
places, and incidents are either the product of the author's
imagination or are used fictitiously.

Library and Archives Canada Cataloguing in Publication

Title: Emily and Sam : the case of the missing turtle / by Dave Cole.
Other titles: Case of the missing turtle
Names: Cole, David, 1957- author. | Mitchell, Matty, illustrator.
Description: Series statement: Emily and Sam series ; book 1 |
"A math adventure." | Illustrated by Matty Mitchell.
Identifiers: Canadiana (print) 20230478131 |
Canadiana (ebook) 2023047814X |
ISBN 9781988761893 (softcover) |
ISBN 9781988761909 (EPUB)
Subjects: LCGFT: Novels.
Classification: LCC PZ7.1.C64 C37 2024 | DDC j813/.6—dc23

Cover Image: Matty Mitchell
Book Design: David Moratto

Printed in Canada
www.CommonDeerPress.com

To Jordan, who always
has a hug for me.

Sam Makes a Discovery

Sam Hilbert skidded his bike to a stop, his tires sliding on the slick pavement.

"Look out!" his twin sister Emily screamed as she swerved to miss him. She stopped her bike on the grass and turned angrily toward her brother.

"What were you doing stopping right in front of me like that?" she asked.

"Come over here and you'll see," Sam said. He got off his bike and bent over to peer at something in the grass by the sidewalk.

Emily put her bike down and walked over slowly. Her brother loved to play tricks on her, so she was careful as she came closer.

"It's not a snake, is it?" Emily hated snakes.

"Better."

She looked over his shoulder and smiled. It wasn't a snake. It was a box turtle. Emily got down on her knees in the wet grass to examine the turtle. It was about five inches across. Its shell was dark brown with splotches of yellow. The turtle was trying to slowly walk away, but Sam put his hand in its path. The turtle immediately ducked its head and legs into its hard shell.

"It's so cute!" Emily exclaimed. "Do you think it's a boy turtle or a girl turtle?"

"I don't know," Sam said. "It's pretty big, so I think it might be a male."

"I bet Mom or Dad would know."

"Probably."

Sam and Emily thought their parents knew just about everything, and if they didn't know something, they always made it a point to help the kids find the information they were looking for.

"Should we take him home?" Sam asked.

"Yes!" Emily answered immediately. "Do you think Mom and Dad will let us keep him?"

"Maybe," Sam said, but he didn't sound very sure of his answer. "Let's take him home and see what they say."

"I have a better idea," Emily said. "Let's not

say anything yet. We can keep the turtle in the basement for a few days while we figure out the best time to ask them."

"Good idea," he agreed.

The turtle stuck his head partway out of his shell and gave a quick peek around. When Sam reached his hand down, the turtle quickly pulled his head back into the shell again.

"It looks like he's a little shy," Sam said.

"Probably scared," Emily replied. "Wouldn't you be if a giant hand came reaching for you?"

Sam laughed. "Yeah, I guess I would."

He opened his backpack and carefully placed the turtle inside next to his binder and lunchbox.

And with that, Sam and Emily became the parents of a box turtle. Whether or not their parents would let them keep him was still to be seen.

What Do Turtles Eat?

"What do you think we should name him?" asked Sam.

"I don't know," Emily replied.

She looked down at the turtle. His head was out, and he was looking around curiously, although there wasn't much to see in his new home in an old cardboard box on the floor in the basement. The turtle took a few steps forward but stopped when he reached one side of the box. He turned to the left and took a few more steps before he came to another wall. He turned again but soon ran into a third wall. He tucked his head back into his shell.

"What do you think he's looking for?" Sam asked.

"Probably food. What do you think turtles eat?"

"Vegetables, I guess."

"Like carrots and lettuce?"

"I think so," Sam said.

"Let's get some different ones from the kitchen and see which ones he likes," Emily said.

"Good idea. We should also get him some water to drink."

They went up the stairs and peeked around the basement door into the kitchen. There was no sign of their parents, so Emily quickly went to the fridge and scooped up some vegetables while her brother filled a shallow bowl with water. They quietly closed the basement door and tiptoed back downstairs.

"Okay, now we'll see what turtles like to eat," said Emily as she arranged three green beans, a small carrot, and two leaves of lettuce on one side of the box. Sam carefully placed the water bowl in a corner. Then they sat back to watch.

For a while, the turtle stayed in his shell. Then, little by little, his head poked out, followed by his legs. The turtle took a few slow steps toward the beans. He pushed one to the side with his head but didn't try any. He ignored the carrot completely. When he got to the lettuce, though, he took a bite and began chewing.

"We have a winner!" Emily said happily. "He likes the lettuce!"

"Yeah, he's really chomping into it," Sam agreed.

"That's it!"

"What's it?"

"His name," Emily said. "How about Chomper?"

Sam thought for a moment and then grinned. "Chomper. I like it."

"What do you think, Chomper?" Emily asked the turtle.

The turtle didn't answer, just kept chewing the lettuce.

"Well, he didn't say no," Sam said.

"That's good enough for me," his sister said. "Chomper it is, then."

"Do we need to make him a bed or something?" Sam asked.

"I don't think so," Emily said thoughtfully. "I mean, he carries his whole house around with him already, doesn't he?"

"I guess that makes sense," Sam said. "We should find out more about turtles, though. Then we'll know how to take good care of him."

"You know where we can go to find out, don't you?" Emily asked.

"Where?"

"The children's zoo!"

A Visit to the Children's Zoo

The next day was a Saturday. The twins got up early and quickly ate their breakfast. The zoo was only a short distance from their house, so it didn't take long for Emily and Sam to ride their bikes there. Most trips to the zoo started with a visit to the elephants and hippos, but this time they went straight to the children's zoo for a visit with their favorite zookeeper.

"Hi Amira!" Emily shouted out as soon as they entered the building.

"Hi Emily. Hi Sam," she said with a smile.

Since the zoo was free and so close to their house, Emily and Sam visited as often as they could. The children's zoo was one of their favorite parts of the zoo because that was

where they could see some of the animals up close and learn all about them. Amira Bashar was in charge of education at the children's zoo and the twins always loved to hear her talk about the animals.

"Do you know anything about box turtles?" Emily asked.

"I do," Amira answered. "In fact, we have a new turtle resident that just came in last week. Let me introduce you to Figure Eight."

"Figure Eight?" Sam said. "That's a strange name for a turtle."

"You'll see why we named her that," Amira said. She led Sam and Emily to the other side of the room. In the middle of the glass enclosure was the strangest looking turtle they had ever seen. Instead of being oval-shaped, the shell was shaped like the number eight.

"Oh!" Sam said. "Now the name makes sense. But why is her shell shaped like that?"

Amira frowned. "When she was little, she got stuck in a ring of plastic used to hold soda cans. For years she just dragged the plastic ring around. Her shell couldn't grow where the plastic ring was, so the middle of her shell stayed the same size while the rest of her shell grew around it. Someone found her and brought her to us. We can't fix the shell, but at least we can make sure she lives a safe, happy life."

"That's really sad," Emily said.

"It is," Amira agreed.

"Is there any way we can help?" Sam asked.

"There is," Amira said. "If you see one of the plastic rings on the ground, pick it up. Use some scissors to cut each of the rings before you throw it away in a garbage can. You can also tell your friends and your parents not to buy products that use plastic rings."

"You can count on me!" Emily said.

"Me too!" Sam chimed in.

"Great!" said Amira. "Now, why do you want to know about box turtles?"

"Well," Sam started, "we kind of have one now."

"Kind of?" Amira asked, crossing her arms.

"We haven't told our parents yet," Emily admitted. "We're waiting for the right time."

Amira smiled. "I'm glad you're going to tell your mom and dad. Box turtles can be great pets, but you need to take good care of them. They're not like dogs or cats, who love to be petted. Turtles do best when you leave them alone. Too much touching can make them very nervous."

"That's good to know," Sam said. "What do they like to eat?"

"Great question! When they are young, like up to age six, they are carnivorous. Do you know what that means?"

"They eat meat, right?" Sam said. "Like a T. rex."

"That's right. In the wild, turtles will eat small animals like fish, frogs, snakes, and birds. They'll even eat larger dead animals. Of course, they also eat vegetables, too, like berries, roots, and flowers."

"We fed Chomper some lettuce today," Emily said.

"Chomper? That's a great name," Amira said. "And lettuce is a great thing to feed him. Here at the zoo, we feed turtles salad, earthworms, and crickets."

Sam wrote *earthworms and crickets* down in the little notebook he always carried in his back pocket.

"What else do we need to know?" Emily asked.

"Hmm," said Amira. "Where are you keeping him?"

"In a cardboard box in the basement," Sam answered.

Amira frowned. "Turtles like lots of sunlight.

That's why we have Figure Eight's enclosure right here by the window. They also need some room to move around."

"Could we just keep him in the backyard?" Sam imagined Chomper enjoying the grassy yard. "He'd have plenty of room, and we have a fence all around the yard so he can't get away."

"No, you'll need an enclosure to protect him," Amira said. "Something like a four-foot by four-foot pen would work great."

"Protect him from what?" Emily asked. "Doesn't his shell already protect him?"

"It does, but dogs and other neighborhood animals could still hurt him if he's not protected," she explained.

Protect him from Biscuit, Sam wrote in his notebook. Biscuit was Sam and Emily's golden retriever. He was very friendly but also got very excited when he saw squirrels and other animals.

Sam and Emily examined Figure Eight's home. There was a small pond on one side. A pile of leaves in a corner looked like a great spot for the turtle to sleep.

Lots of sunlight. Four-foot by four-foot pen, Sam noted.

"Any more advice?" Emily asked.

Amira thought for a moment and then put one hand on each of their shoulders. "Having a pet is a big responsibility," she said. "You must remember to take good care of Chomper every day. My advice is to let your parents know about your new pet and make sure they're okay with it."

Emily nodded. "We will. We just need to find the perfect time to tell them."

Can We Keep Him?

It turns out, the perfect time came just as they got home. The mail truck was pulling away from their house as they arrived. Sam brought his bike up to the mailbox and pulled out a handful of envelopes.

"Oh! It's our progress reports!" he announced.

"Great!" Emily replied. "I think mine will be really good."

"I bet mine is even better," Sam said.

"Yeah? We'll see about that! Anyway, let's show them to Mom and Dad and introduce them to Chomper."

They burst into the house. "Our progress reports are here!" Emily yelled.

Their mom was smiling as she came into

the kitchen. "Well, they must be good if you're so excited about them."

The twins grinned from ear to ear. Both were good students and got along well with their teacher, Mrs. Gunther.

"Open them up," Sam urged.

"Open what up?" asked their dad as he joined everyone in the kitchen.

"Our progress reports!" Emily said, barely containing her excitement.

"Hmm, they must be good if you're so anxious to open them," he said.

Emily laughed. "That's what Mom said."

"Well, I suppose we should open them, huh?" Mom asked.

"Or we could wait until after dinner," Dad teased.

"No, now," Sam pleaded.

Their dad saw the earnest expression on their faces and gave in. "Okay, let's see what we've got."

He opened the first envelope and pulled out a single sheet of paper. He looked over the report without saying a word. He handed it to his wife while he opened the second envelope. Again, there was a single sheet of paper, which he examined quietly.

Now the twins were getting a little worried. They had been expecting big smiles from their parents, but neither had changed their expression. Finally, their father looked at both kids.

"Is this the best you could do?" he asked. Emily's face fell. What had gone wrong? She and Sam paid attention in class and always turned in their homework.

"Your teacher marked VG in all of your subjects," their dad said. "Does that mean very giggly or very goofy?"

"VG means very good!" the twins shouted.

"Oh, that makes more sense," he said. "I guess these are pretty good reports then."

Both parents broke into wide grins as they handed the papers to the kids.

"Okay, you fooled us," Emily admitted as she checked out her progress report.

"Yeah, you got us good," Sam agreed.

"Great work, you two," their mom said. "We should find some way to celebrate. What do you think we should do?"

Emily gave Sam a long look. He nodded.

Emily took a deep breath and said, "Well, there is something we'd like to ask you."

A few minutes later, their parents had met

Chomper and had agreed to let the kids keep him.

"On one condition," their dad said. "You two have to agree to take very good care of Chomper."

"We will!" they agreed.

"We're going to build a pen in the backyard so no animals can get to him," Sam said.

"And that includes you, Biscuit!" Emily said to the dog. Biscuit just cocked his head to one side and looked at her.

"Can you help us build it?" Sam asked them.

"How about I supply the tools and materials and you two do all the building?" their dad countered.

"Deal," the twins said in unison.

"Okay, then let me know what I need to pick up from the hardware store."

"Come on, Sam, let's start planning!" Emily said.

Designing a Home for Chomper

"How do you think we should build the pen?" Sam asked. He and his sister were working at the kitchen table while they munched on some grapes.

"I was thinking we could put poles in the ground and then some kind of fence stuff around the edges," said Emily. "We could attach the fence to the poles."

She drew a picture of what she was imagining.

"Yeah, that looks like it would work," Sam said.

"How big did Amira say we needed to make the pen?" Emily asked.

Sam looked at his notebook. "Four feet by four feet."

"We could put a pole every foot. That would make it harder for animals to get in."

"That sounds good," Sam said. "That means we would need four poles for each side, right?"

Emily thought for a moment, then shook her head. "I don't think that's right."

Sam looked up in surprise. "It isn't?"

Emily took a handful of grapes and began laying them out on the table. She started with four grapes in a line.

"Let's say these grapes are the poles," she said. "If there is one foot between each of the grapes, that would only be three feet altogether."

Sam counted to make sure his sister was right. Then he added another grape to the line and counted again. "You're right," he said. "We need five poles on each side."

"So, if the pen has four sides, and each side needs five poles, that means we would need twenty poles," Emily calculated.

"We should start a list of stuff we need Dad to buy." Sam turned to a new page in his notebook and began making their shopping list.

20 poles

"How much of the fence stuff do you think we'll need?" Sam asked.

"Well," said Emily, "if each side is four feet long, and there are four sides . . ."

"Sixteen feet! Right," Sam said. He added this to the list.

20 poles
16 feet of fence

"And some way to attach the fence to the poles," Emily added. "Maybe some rope or something."

Sam added this to the list.

20 poles
16 feet of fence
Something to attach fence to the poles

"Is that everything?" he asked.

Emily thought for a moment. "I think so. We have enough lettuce in the fridge and I don't think Biscuit will mind if Chomper used one of his old water bowls."

They took the list and Emily's drawing to their father. He examined the list and nodded. "Okay," he said. "I can pick up the building materials this afternoon."

Two hours later, their dad returned with his car trunk filled. Emily and Sam raced to the end of the driveway to meet him.

"Here you go," he said. "Poles, fencing, and some tie wraps to attach the fencing to the poles." He handed Emily a canvas tote bag.

"What's in here?" Emily asked.

"Some hinges so you can make a gate if you want. I also got a hook to secure the gate so animals can't get in."

"Thanks, Dad!" Sam said. "Come on, Emily, let's get started."

They unloaded the supplies and carried them to the backyard.

"Okay, where should we build the pen?" Emily asked.

"How about we put it next to the deck," Sam said. "That will make it easier to feed Chomper because he'll be closer to the kitchen."

"Good idea," said Emily. "Let's lay the poles out on the ground first."

They used a one-foot-long ruler to help them put the poles in the right place. They formed a square and put five poles on each side, just like they had planned. But wait, something was wrong! They had four poles left over!

"What did we do wrong?" Emily asked. "We need five poles on each side, right?"

"Right," Sam agreed.

"And five plus five plus five plus five equals twenty, right?"

"Right."

"Then why do we have four poles left over?"

Sam looked at the square they had laid out, thought for a moment, and then yelled out, "The corners!"

"What about the corners?" Emily asked.

"Each corner pole is on two different sides," Sam explained, "so they really count twice. That means we don't really need twenty poles. We only need sixteen."

He drew a picture in his notebook so Emily could see what he was talking about.

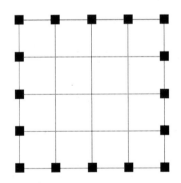

"Oh! I get it now," Emily said. "I guess we're going to end up with some extra poles."

"Maybe not," said a voice behind them. They turned to see their dad standing on the deck. He had come out to check on their progress.

"What do you mean?" Emily asked.

"Well, the hardware store sold the fencing material in lengths of twenty feet, so you've also got an extra four feet of fence."

"Wait a minute," Sam said. "That means we can build a bigger pen if we want!"

"Yeah!" said Emily.

What's the Best Design?

"Let's draw the different sizes and shapes we can make for Chomper's pen," said Emily.

Sam turned to a new page in his notebook. "We could just make it longer," he said. "We have four extra poles so we could make it two feet longer."

He drew his idea in his notebook and showed it to his sister.

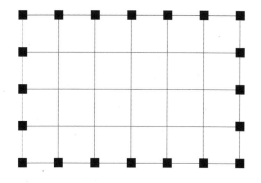

Emily counted the poles: there were seven on each of the long sides and three on the short sides, if you didn't count the corner poles again.

"That's seven plus seven is fourteen poles for the long sides," she said, "plus another six on the short sides. That's twenty. Perfect!"

"We also need to check if we have enough fencing for this design," her brother pointed out. "There are two sides of six feet and two sides of four feet, so that makes twelve feet total for the long sides and eight feet for the short sides. Twelve plus eight is twenty, so we have just enough. Let's build it!"

"Is that the best shape we can make?" Emily asked.

"What do you mean?" Sam asked.

"I counted the squares and there are twenty-four in this design. That's bigger than the sixteen squares in the four-by-four pen we were originally building. But maybe we can make an even bigger pen if we change the lengths of the sides."

"Okay," Sam asked. "How?"

"Well, what if we made it even longer?"

Emily drew her idea in her brother's notebook.

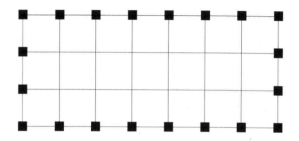

Sam counted the poles. "That's a total of sixteen poles for the long sides and another four for the short sides. That's twenty, alright."

"How about the fencing?" Emily asked. She counted the length of all the sides, and it came to exactly twenty. "There's enough fencing too."

"Okay, how many squares does Chomper have now?" Sam asked.

Emily counted and frowned. "Only twenty-one," she said. "My design made things worse."

"I have an idea," said Sam. "What if we put all the different numbers into a table chart, like we did with the data for our class science fair project?"

The class project was to figure out which lollypop flavor would last the longest. The kids in the class did the experiment by licking different flavors to see how many licks it took until the candy was completely gone. They weren't very good testers since some of the kids crunched up the lollypops when they got near the end. While they never learned what flavor took the most licks, they did learn how to put their data into a chart to help them compare results.

"Good idea," Emily said. "We could put the number of poles, the length and width of the sides, the total length of the fence, and the number of squares of pen space for Chomper. It will make it easy to see which design is the best."

Sam quickly drew a chart in his trusty notebook and filled in the first few rows with what they had already learned.

Number of Poles	Width	Length	Length of Fence	Squares of Pen Space
16	4	4	16	16
20	4	6	20	24
20	3	7	20	21

Sam looked at the table and quickly spotted something. "Look! The length of the fence is always equal to the number of poles."

Emily thought for a moment. "I guess it makes sense. There is one foot of fencing between every two poles."

"But how come the length of the fence isn't one foot shorter?" Sam asked. "I mean, if I only had two poles, I'd only need one foot of fencing between the two."

"Yeah, but that's for a straight line. If we made a triangle with three poles, we would need three feet of fencing. Since our shape goes all the way around, it will finish up at the same place it started. The last foot of fencing connects back to the first pole."

"Oh! I get it," Sam said. "Okay, what shape should we try next?"

"What if we turned one of these a different direction?" Emily asked. "Like, instead of four feet long and six feet wide, we make it six feet long and four feet wide?"

Sam thought for a moment and then added this new shape to his table.

Number of Poles	Width	Length	Length of Fence	Squares of Pen Space
16	4	4	16	16
20	4	6	20	24
20	3	7	20	21
20	6	4	20	24

"It's exactly the same as the other one," Emily said.

"Of course," Sam said. "All we're really doing is turning the same shape around, so nothing changes." He demonstrated what he meant by turning his notebook to show the two shapes were really the same.

Emily nodded. "Yeah, that makes sense. Let's maybe try something different. These have all been just different-sized rectangles."

"You're right," Sam said. "The table shows that making it longer and skinnier makes the pen space smaller, so maybe we should try to go shorter and fatter. What do you think about this one?"

Sam turned to a new page and drew his new design.

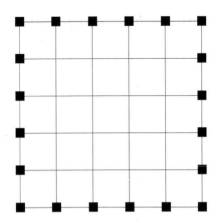

"That's just another rectangle," Emily said.

"Yeah, but it's also a square," Sam replied.

They quickly counted the poles, the lengths of each side, and the number of squares. Sam added them to his table.

Number of Poles	Width	Length	Length of Fence	Squares of Pen Space
16	4	4	16	16
20	4	6	20	24
20	3	7	20	21
20	6	4	20	24
20	5	5	20	25

"I think we may have found a winner," Sam said with a smile. "If we make it a square, it uses the same number of poles and length of fence but gives Chomper the biggest pen."

Emily studied the table. "It may be the biggest," she agreed, "but is it the best?"

"Why wouldn't the biggest be the best?" Sam asked.

"Well, I was thinking, what is Chomper going to do when it rains?"

"We could put a cover on his pen," Sam said.

"But then he won't get the sunlight that Amira says he needs."

"Good point."

"What if we only covered part of the pen?" Emily asked.

"That could work," he replied.

"I think I might have an idea," Emily said.

She turned to the next page of Sam's notebook and drew another design.

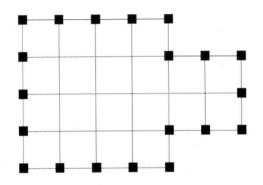

"It uses exactly twenty poles and twenty feet of fencing," she said.

"But it only has twenty squares of pen space," Sam said. "That's less than the square one."

"Yeah, but that's still more than Amira said he needed," Emily said. "And we can cover this extra area, so Chomper has a protected place for his food and water."

Sam looked at the design. A wide grin spread across his face. "I love it! Let's start building!"

Chomper Moves In

The twins worked on the pen for two hours without a break. Their dad showed them how to use a hammer to pound the poles into the ground and how to make a gate with the hinges. Their mom showed them how to use the tie wraps to connect the fencing to the poles.

"Finished!" Sam exclaimed as he secured a piece of wood over Chomper's eating area.

Sam and Emily stood back to admire their work. The pen was three feet tall and had a small gate on one side that would allow them to put out food and water for the turtle.

"It looks great!" Emily said. "But now for the real test. Does Chomper like it?"

"Let's go get him and see."

Emily carefully carried Chomper up the stairs and out to his new home. They had already filled his water bowl and put out a plate of lettuce for him. She opened the pen gate and placed their new pet in the enclosure. Then she stepped out to give Chomper a chance to look around. She and Sam watched him anxiously.

Chomper poked his head out of his shell. He looked left and right before slowly putting his legs out. He immediately walked to the plate of lettuce and took a couple of small bites.

"I think we picked the right name for him," Sam said. "He sure does like to eat."

"I think he likes his new home," Emily said happily as Chomper began to take a tour of his new home. He finally settled into one corner of the pen and pulled back into his shell.

"He's probably taking a nap," Sam said.

"Who's taking a nap?" came a voice from behind them. They turned to see Mateo Lopez, their friend and next-door neighbor, standing in their backyard. He was trying to look over their shoulders into the pen.

"Chomper," Emily said.

"Who's Chomper?" Mateo asked.

"Our new box turtle," Sam answered. "We

just finished building his new pen." Sam stepped aside so Mateo could have a better look.

"Cool," Mateo said. "Can I touch it?"

"Amira said we shouldn't touch him very much" Emily said. "Box turtles are kind of shy."

"Who's Amira?"

"She works in the children's zoo," she said. "She told us all about taking care of Chomper."

Mateo got down on his hands and knees next to the corner of the pen near the turtle.

"What are you doing?" asked Sam.

"Waiting to see if it'll come out of its shell," Mateo said. "Did you know its neck is shaped like an S? That's how it can put its whole head into its shell."

"Chomper isn't an *it*," Emily said. "He's a *he*."

"How do you know it's a boy?" he asked.

"We don't really know he's a boy," Sam admitted. "But we think he is because he's pretty big and male turtles get bigger than females."

Mateo got even closer to the edge of the pen. Chomper stuck his head out and looked right at Mateo.

"It's a male, alright," Mateo said.

"How do you know," asked Emily.

"It has red eyes. Males have red eyes and females have brown eyes."

"Wow, you know a lot about box turtles," Sam said.

"Yeah, I always wanted one," Mateo said sadly, "but my parents wouldn't let me. My mom thinks turtles are just snakes with legs."

Emily giggled at the thought of a snake walking. She didn't like snakes, and she didn't think Chomper was anything like a snake.

"Well, I guess I'd better get going," Mateo said as he rose to his feet. He took one last look at the turtle, then he wiped the grass off his knees and walked toward his house.

"You can come visit Chomper whenever you want," Sam called after him.

"He really seems to like turtles," Emily said.

"Yeah, he does," Sam said. "You want to go play some cards?"

"Sure," she said. "See you later, Chomper."

Chomper Is Gone!

The next morning, the sun peeked through the drapes and into Emily's eyes. She blinked a few times and then bounded out of bed. She dressed quickly and hurried to the kitchen, where she almost ran into her mother as she rounded the corner.

"Whoa! Someone is in a hurry this morning," her mom laughed.

"I've got to check on Chomper," Emily explained.

"Well, I'm glad to see you and your brother are taking good care of your new pet," her mom said.

Emily slid open the glass patio door and stepped out onto the deck. She peered over the railing and gasped. The gate to the pen was halfway open. She ran to the pen and looked in, but she already knew: Chomper was gone!

"Mom! Dad! Sam!" she howled.

Her mother rushed out of the house. "What is it?" she asked in alarm.

"Chomper is gone!"

"Gone? What do you mean?"

"I mean he's gone. He's not here."

"Take a breath," her mom said. "Are you sure he's not in the pen?"

"He's not," Emily said. "I looked everywhere. And the gate was open when I got here."

"Did you or your brother maybe accidentally leave it open?"

"No!" Emily insisted. "I even checked the little hook on the gate before I went to bed last night. The gate was closed."

"What's with all the noise?" Sam asked as he stepped onto the deck in his pajamas.

"Chomper is gone!" Emily said.

"What do you mean, gone?"

"Why does everyone keep asking me that? Gone means he's not here," Emily said. A tear slipped from one eye and ran down her cheek.

"But where did he go?" her brother asked.

"How should I know?" Emily said. "Like I

told Mom, I checked the gate before I went to bed last night. Now the gate is open, and Chomper is gone."

"Okay, now let's all settle down," said their dad as he joined them on the deck. "Could he have gotten under the fence?"

"He didn't need to if the gate was open," Sam said.

"Well, he couldn't have wandered off too far," their dad said. "I'll help you search after breakfast."

"Can we search now?" Emily asked.

"After breakfast," her father repeated. It was Sunday, which meant the family would all eat breakfast together.

Emily didn't have much of an appetite because she was so worried about the turtle. Sam said he wasn't hungry either but still ate two bowls of cereal and drank a large glass of juice.

"I'm going to run up and get dressed," he said when he had finished.

He was back in two minutes, and they began the search. They searched the backyard for more than an hour, but there was no sign of Chomper anywhere.

"I'm sorry, kids," their dad said. "It looks like your new pet is gone."

"But we have to keep searching!" Emily said.

"He's got to be out here somewhere," Sam agreed.

"Okay, you can keep looking, but I've got some things I need to do," their dad said. He walked back into the house.

"How could Chomper have run off like that?" Emily asked.

"He couldn't have," her brother replied. "You checked the gate, right?"

"Right. I even wiggled it to make sure the little hook was secure."

"And the gate was open when you went out this morning?"

"Yeah, it was open four or five inches," she said.

"Then someone had to have opened it," he said.

Emily gasped. "Mateo!"

"Maybe," Sam said. "He was pretty interested in Chomper, wasn't he?"

"He definitely was," Emily agreed, "and he said he always wanted to have a box turtle. I bet he came over here after we went to bed and took him out of the pen."

"But he's our friend," Sam said. "Do you really think it was him?"

"I don't know who else could have done it," Emily said. "It had to be him."

"So how are we going to get Chomper back? We can't just go ask Mateo. He'll just say he didn't do it."

"Then we'll have to find a way to catch him with Chomper," Emily said. "We can't let him get away with this!"

Trailing Mateo

Sam and Emily moped on the front porch the rest of the morning. They had tried to come up with a plan to catch Mateo with their turtle, but so far they hadn't come up with anything.

"I'll be back later, Mom," came a loud voice from next door. It was Mateo!

The twins watched as their neighbor wheeled his bike from his garage and set off down the street.

"Come on!" Emily said. "Let's follow him."

"You tell Mom and Dad and I'll get the bikes," Sam said.

Mateo was just rounding the corner at the end of the street when they mounted their bikes. They pedaled furiously to catch up.

"Hurry!" Emily said. "We can't let him get away."

Sam rode up beside her and they turned the corner. Luckily, Mateo didn't seem to be in too big of a hurry, so they were able to catch up with him.

"Not too close," Sam said to his sister. "We don't want him to know we're following him."

They trailed Mateo at a distance until he turned onto Main Street. When the twins came around the corner, Mateo was parking his bike on a rack in front of a grocery store.

"There he is," Emily said. "I bet he's getting food for Chomper."

"You might be right," Sam said. "Let's go in and see what he's buying."

They leaned their bikes against the side wall of the store and walked in. Sam pulled his hoodie up so Mateo wouldn't recognize him. Emily picked up a page of store ads and used it to hide her face. They watched Mateo from the end of an aisle. He went straight to the produce section and selected a head of lettuce.

"I knew it!" Emily said angrily. "He's buying lettuce for *our* turtle!"

"It sure looks like it," Sam said. "Let's go tell

him we know what he did." He started toward Mateo, but Emily grabbed his arm and pulled him back.

"Not yet," she whispered. "We need to catch him with Chomper."

"That lettuce is all the evidence I need."

"He's just going to say that he didn't do it. Then what?"

Sam thought for a moment, then slowly nodded. "Okay, let's keep watching him."

They peeked around the corner of the dairy aisle as Mateo paid and walked out with a reusable bag clutched in one hand.

"Let's go," Emily said as soon as Mateo left.

When they got to the exit, their friend had already gotten back on his bike and was pedaling away.

"Now where is he going?" wondered Sam.

"I don't know, but it doesn't look like he's headed home," Emily said.

The twins got on their bikes and followed Mateo as he pedaled further down Main Street. But he didn't go very far. Just down the block, Mateo parked his bike and entered another store.

"It's the pet store," Sam said. "Now what's he buying?"

"I'm going to find out," Emily said. "You stay out here while I go in."

Emily peeked in the front door of the pet store but saw no sign of Mateo. She slipped in and spotted him looking over the top of a large crate of dirt. As she watched, he dug his hand in and pulled out a handful of earthworms and dumped them into a bag.

"I knew it!" she said to herself. She snuck back out and found her brother standing by their bikes in an alley next to the pet store.

"He's buying worms," Emily told him.

"Worms? Why is he buying worms?"

"Don't you remember what Amira said? Earthworms are one of the things she feeds to Figure Eight."

"That's right," Sam said. "Mateo must be buying worms to feed Chomper. We've got to—"

"Look out!" Emily interrupted. "Here he comes."

Mateo came out of the store with another tote bag. He dangled one bag from each of his bike's handlebars and then mounted the bike. He began pedaling back toward home. As he passed the alley, he didn't notice Sam and Emily ducking behind their bikes.

"Let's follow him home," Sam said.

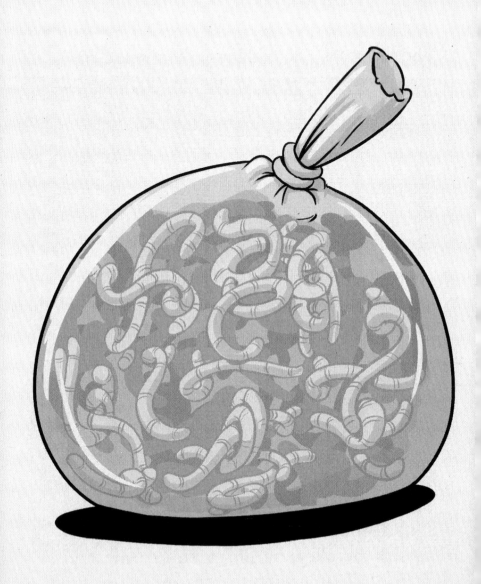

They waited for Mateo to get a little head start and then pedaled after him. Once he reached his house, Sam and Emily saw him drop his bike onto the grass next to his driveway. He took a quick look around and then entered the garage through a side door. When he didn't come back out, the twins crept to the side of Mateo's house and peeked through a dirty garage window.

Mateo was pulling earthworms from the bag and dropping them one by one into a large cardboard box.

"That has to be where he's keeping Chomper," said Emily.

"We have to get our hands on that box," said Sam.

As they watched, Mateo closed the lid on the box, wiped the dirt off his hands, and entered his house through the garage.

"Now's our chance!" Sam said. "Let's go get Chomper."

He tried to turn the knob for the garage door. It was locked.

"Now what do we do?" Sam asked. "Do you think we could pick the lock on the door?"

"What do you know about picking a lock?" Emily asked.

"I don't know, it looks pretty easy when they do it on TV."

"Well, this is real life. Besides, we don't have any tools even if we did know how to do it."

"How about this for a tool?" Sam asked. He lifted a large rock from the side of the house.

"What are you going to do with that?"

"We could break the window."

"You don't think Mateo and his parents would hear us smashing their window?" Emily asked.

Sam dropped the rock to the ground. "Yeah, I guess I didn't think about that."

Emily thought for a moment, then tried lifting the garage window. It was heavy, but she was able to raise it a couple of inches.

"I don't think we need a rock." She smiled. "The window isn't locked."

"Great!" said Sam. "Let's get it open and I'll crawl in and grab the box."

Working together, they pushed the window up several more inches, but that was as far as it would go.

"I don't think you'll be able to fit through there," Emily said, "but I think I could squeeze through. Boost me up."

"No, not now," Sam said. He looked around.

"It's daytime. Someone might see us. We'll have to come back when it's dark."

"But we can't do it tonight," Emily complained. "We still have homework to do."

Sam agreed. "Let's plan on doing it tomorrow night."

Making a Plan to Rescue Chomper

"Hey Emily!" Mateo called out the next morning as he wheeled his bike in front of Sam and Emily's house.

Emily looked up in surprise. She could not believe Mateo was being so friendly to them after stealing their turtle.

"Yeah, what do you want?" she asked in an icy tone.

"You guys want to ride to school with me this morning?" Mateo asked.

"No."

Now Mateo looked surprised. "How come?" he asked.

"Um, I'm waiting for my brother."

Just then Sam came out on the front porch. He looked at Mateo and then back at his sister.

"What's he doing here?" Sam whispered.

"He wants to ride to school with us," Emily answered quietly.

"Are you kidding me?"

"No, he's acting like nothing happened."

"Well, I'm not riding with him," Sam said.

"You guys coming or not?" Mateo asked.

"No, I forgot my backpack," Sam answered.

"Have you checked your back?" Mateo asked with a laugh.

Sure enough, Sam was wearing it. "I mean, I forgot to put my homework in my backpack," he said. "You go on without us."

Mateo gave Sam a long look, then shrugged his shoulders and pedaled away.

"Can you believe that guy?" Emily fumed. "He steals our turtle and then acts like we're still friends."

"We'll see how he feels tonight once he finds out we took Chomper back," Sam said. "Come on, we'd better get to school."

"Aren't you forgetting something?" Emily asked.

"I don't think so," Sam replied.

"Didn't you tell Mateo you had to go back in and get your homework?" Emily teased.

The school day seemed to last forever. Sam and Emily couldn't concentrate on anything. Sam missed two easy addition problems during math group. Mrs. Gunther had to ask Emily to pay attention several times. All the twins could think about was how they were going to rescue Chomper that evening.

The dismissal bell finally rang, and they ran to their bikes. They both pedaled furiously until they were gasping for breath. As soon as they got home, they went straight to their rooms to do their homework. They didn't want anything to get in the way of their nighttime mission.

"No snack?" their dad called up the stairs.

"Not hungry," Sam yelled back.

"Me neither," Emily yelled. "We've got lots of homework."

As soon as they had finished their homework, they met in Emily's room to discuss their plan.

"Okay, here's what I've got," Sam said, consulting his trusty notebook. "First, we have to figure out a reason for us to leave the house after dinner."

"I think I have an idea," Emily said. "What if we told Mom and Dad that I have to take some homework to Yasmin?"

"Why would you be taking her homework?"

"Because she was sick today."

"No, she wasn't. She was . . . Oh, I get it. We just *tell* them she was sick."

"Exactly," Emily said.

"But why would I go with you? She's your friend, not mine."

"Because I don't want to walk there by myself in the dark."

"That makes sense," Sam said. He made a note in his book. "Okay, first, we tell them we have some homework to take to Yasmin. Second, we sneak over to Mateo's house and make sure the coast is clear. Third, you go in the garage window and grab the box where he's keeping Chomper. Fourth, you unlock the garage door."

"Why can't I just come back out the window?" Emily asked.

"I don't think the box will fit."

"Good point," she said. "What if I just get Chomper?"

"We want the box because it is evidence that Mateo stole him."

"It's a good plan," Emily said. "It almost seems too simple. What if something goes wrong?"

"What could go wrong?" Sam asked.

As it turned out, there was a lot that could go wrong.

The Plan Goes All Wrong

After they had completed their plan, Emily went downstairs to begin working on step one.

"Mom, can I take some homework over to Yasmin's house after dinner?" Emily asked.

"Oh," her mother frowned. "Was she out today?"

Emily gulped. The twins didn't usually lie to their parents. "Yeah, I think she was sick," Emily replied.

"Sure, honey, I can drive you over right now if you want," her mom said. "The chicken needs to bake for another thirty minutes."

"Um ... it's um ... not quite ready yet," Emily stammered.

"It's not ready?"

"Yeah," Emily said, thinking fast. "Mrs. Gunther asked me to add a few notes to the homework first."

"Okay," her mom said. "I can drive you over after dinner."

"Can't I just walk over?"

"It's two blocks and it will be getting dark, won't it?"

"Yeah, but Sam can go with me," Emily said.

Her mom thought about this with her hands on her hips. "Okay, but I want you to come right back."

"We will, Mom. We'll be really fast, and me and Sam already finished our homework," Emily said.

Her mom looked up in surprise. "Sam finished his homework without me reminding him?"

"Yeah," Emily said, shrugging. "It was just math and some reading for social studies."

"You know," her mom said as she pulled her cell phone out of her pocket. "I should give Yasmin's mom a call and ask how she's doing."

"You can't!" Emily blurted out. When her mom gave her a puzzled look, she continued. "I mean, you can't because her mom is out of town. That's why I'm taking Yasmin's homework to her instead of her mom picking it up."

74

Before her mom could say anything else, Emily darted out of the kitchen. Up in Sam's room a moment later, she breathed a sigh of relief. "Whew, I almost blew it. Mom wanted to drive me over to Yasmin's house."

"What did you say?" Sam asked.

"I told her Yasmin's mom was out of town and that you would walk with me," she explained. "I hate lying to her but it's the only way they'll let us out of the house."

"They'd understand if they knew we were rescuing Chomper," Sam said. He put a checkmark in his notebook next to step one of their plan. "We're ready for step two, sneaking to Mateo's house."

At dinner, the twins wolfed down their food, anxious to get on with their rescue plan.

"Are you two extra hungry tonight or was dinner extra delicious?" their mom asked as she looked at their empty plates.

"Extra hungry," Sam said.

"Extra delicious," Emily added. "Can we go to Yasmin's house now?"

Their mom nodded and the twins raced up the stairs. Emily gathered up a handful of papers and the twins went back downstairs.

"We're going," Emily called out to her mom.

"Tell her I hope she's feeling better," her mom replied.

"I will!" Emily said before she and Sam walked out the front door.

When they got to the sidewalk, Emily turned right.

"Where are you going?" Sam asked. "Mateo's house is the other direction."

"We're supposed to be going to Yasmin's house, remember?"

"Oh, yeah," Sam said. "Good thinking."

"We can circle around the block so we'll be gone for long enough that Mom and Dad won't be suspicious," Emily said.

It was getting dark by the time they approached Mateo's house. There was light coming from several windows, but the garage was dark.

"Looks like the coast is clear," Sam said as he peeked around the front of the house. The two faded back into the shadows on the side of the garage.

"Help me with this window," Emily said.

They quietly raised the window and, with a little help from her brother, Emily was able to squeeze through the narrow space. It was pitch black in the garage.

"We should have brought a flashlight," she whispered to her brother. "I can't see anything."

"Well, whatever you do, don't knock anything—" he began, but it was too late!

Emily tripped over something heavy and oddly shaped. A loud crash echoed through the garage as whatever it was slammed against the wall. Pieces of metal, maybe tools, clattered to the concrete floor. Emily couldn't have made any more noise if she had tried.

She heard footsteps from inside the house. There was no time to get out of the garage, so she ducked under a plastic tarp. She wedged herself next to something made of metal. It had a faint smell of gasoline. She heard the door from the house to the garage open and a wedge of light appeared under the tarp. Someone was in the garage!

An Unwelcome Surprise

"Who's in here?" yelled a man. It must have been Mr. Lopez.

"What is it?" asked a woman's voice, Mrs. Lopez's. They both must have been standing in the doorway to the garage. "Do you see anything?"

"It looks like the ladder fell down," Mr. Lopez said. From her hiding place under the tarp, Emily could hear Mr. Lopez's footsteps as he walked over to the other side of the garage. "The window is open. I guess maybe the wind blew it over."

"Well, come back to dinner," Mrs. Lopez said. "You can clean up the mess later."

"I should let Mateo clean it up if he was the one who left the window open."

"Come in, the food is getting cold."

"Let me get the window shut first," he said. He closed the window and latched it shut.

"At least the ladder didn't land on my motorcycle," he said. He gave the top of the tarp a pat. Beneath the cover, Emily held her breath.

Finally, Mr. Lopez's footsteps faded, the door to the house opened and closed, and the light went off. Emily silently counted to sixty to make sure he wasn't coming back, then slowly crept out from beneath the tarp.

Emily tried to figure out where she was in the garage. She was afraid to step in any direction because she didn't know what was in her path. She reached her hands out carefully in front of her. Not feeling anything, she took a small step forward. She reached again. There was nothing there, so she took another small step. Slowly but surely, she made her way to the wall of the garage and worked along the wall until she got to the outside door.

She felt around until she found the deadbolt lock. She silently turned the lock until she heard a click, then carefully twisted the doorknob. Trying not to make a sound, she eased the door toward her and slipped through to the outside. She pulled the door shut and took a deep breath.

Then a hand firmly grasped her arm. She tried to scream but all that came out was a small squeak.

"Quiet!" Sam whispered. "Where's the box?"

"I didn't have time to look for it," she said. "I knocked something over and Mr. Lopez came out."

"How did he not see you?"

"I hid under a tarp."

"We have to go back in and get the box," Sam said.

"I'm not going in there," Emily protested. "I almost got caught!"

"We're so close," he insisted. "The door's unlocked now. I'll go in."

"But what if he comes back out while you're in there?" she asked. "Do you know how much trouble we would be in?"

"You're right," he agreed. "We need a diversion."

"Like what?"

"The doorbell," Sam said. "You ring the doorbell and run. While they're answering the door, I'll grab the box."

"No, you should be the one to ring the bell,"

Emily said. "You run a lot faster than me. You ring the bell and I'll get the box."

"Alright, but be careful this time," he said.

"I will," she promised.

"Okay, I'm going to count to thirty and then ring the bell. Get in and out fast!"

Emily nodded. She was scared but knew what she had to do. She counted down silently from thirty, turned the knob, and opened the door a few inches. In the small sliver of moonlight let in through the open door, she saw the cardboard box. She took a deep breath and then raced into the garage. She grasped the box firmly, then ran back outside and closed the door behind her. She listened carefully but didn't hear anything. The garage light remained off. She had made it!

She paused a moment to let Chomper know he was safe. She lifted the lid, poked her head into the box—and screamed!

It wasn't a box turtle. It was a snake! She threw the box and ran.

Mateo Explains

"**What do you** mean it was a snake?" Sam asked.

Sam and Emily were walking back to their house, circling the block to make it seem like they were coming from Yasmin's house.

"I got the box and got out of the garage. I looked in to check on Chomper," Emily explained, "only it wasn't Chomper—it was a snake."

"What did you do?"

"What do you think I did? I dropped the box and took off running. You know I hate snakes!" She shuddered as she thought of her face-to-face meeting with the snake.

"Does that mean Mateo didn't steal Chomper?" asked Sam.

"I don't know," she answered. "I just know when I looked in the box, Chomper wasn't in it."

"But if he didn't steal him, who did?"

They had just reached their front porch when they saw Mateo crossing the yard toward them.

"Hey Mateo. What's up?" Sam asked, pretending he didn't know.

"Did you two take my snake?" he asked. His face was red with anger.

"Your snake?" Sam said. He and Emily quickly looked at each other. "What are you talking about?"

"Someone snuck into our garage and stole my snake."

"What makes you think it was us?" Emily asked.

"Because you left this behind," Mateo said. He was holding up a sheet of paper. Emily recognized it as the fake homework they were supposed to be taking to Yasmin. It had Emily's name at the top of it. She went pale.

"So, it *is* yours," Mateo said. "I found it next to the box I was using to keep the snake. And now he's gone."

Emily looked down. "I'm sorry, Mateo, but I

promise we weren't trying to steal your snake. I hate snakes. They're dangerous."

Mateo snorted. "Dangerous? It was a harmless garter snake."

"It stuck it's tongue out like it was getting ready to bite me."

"That's how snakes smell," Mateo said, "and he wasn't going to take a bite out of you unless maybe he thought you were a tasty worm."

"Worms?" Sam said. "Snakes eat worms?"

"Yeah, I bought some the other day at—"

"—the pet store," Sam finished.

"How'd you know that?" Mateo asked.

"We followed you," Sam admitted.

"Why?"

"Well, you were really interested in Chomper and then the next day he went missing. We thought maybe you took him," Emily said.

"Then we saw you buying lettuce and worms, so we figured you were buying food to feed him," Sam added.

"Snakes don't eat lettuce," Mateo said. "That was for my dad to make a salad for dinner. The earthworms were for the snake, though. Garter snakes love worms and grubs."

"That explains a lot," Emily said. "We looked through your garage window and saw you putting worms in the box, and we thought you were feeding Chomper. We decided to steal him back from you."

"Emily snuck into your garage and grabbed the box, but she dropped it when she saw the snake."

"Dropped it? I threw it!" Emily said. "Did I mention I hate snakes?"

"Only about a hundred times," Sam said. "Hey Mateo, we're really sorry for thinking you stole Chomper."

"Don't worry about it," Mateo said. "I guess the clues did point to me."

"And I'm sorry I made you lose your snake," Emily said. "Do you think you'll be able to find him?"

"Probably not," Mateo said. "But that's okay. My parents never would have let me keep him anyway. Besides, there are lots of garter snakes in yards this time of year, so I can always catch another one."

"Good," Sam said.

"Wait! Are you saying those snakes are everywhere?" Emily said. "I'm never going in the yard again."

Mateo laughed. "I'm sorry you guys lost Chomper," he said.

"Yeah," Emily said. "I'm going to miss that little guy."

"Well, I guess I'd better get home," Mateo said.

"Okay, see you tomorrow," Sam said. "You want to ride to school with us?"

"Sure," Mateo said. "See you tomorrow."

Biscuit to the Rescue

The next day, Sam and Emily were having rainbow chocolate chip cookies as an afterschool snack on the deck.

"I guess we'll never figure out who stole Chomper," Sam said as he grabbed another cookie.

"Probably not," his sister agreed. "If it wasn't Mateo, I don't have any idea who might have done it."

The sliding glass door slid open and a flash of gold bounded past them.

"Hey, Biscuit!" Emily yelled as the dog ran in a large circle around the backyard.

Biscuit looked up at Emily's voice, then ran

to the far corner of the yard and began barking furiously.

"What is it, Biscuit?" Emily called.

Biscuit looked in her direction, then started sniffing through a pile of leaves. Lifting his head, he resumed his frantic barking.

"Biscuit, be quiet!" Sam yelled.

The dog continued to bark and scratch at the leaves.

"I'm going to go see what he found," Emily said. She popped the last cookie in her mouth and walked back to the edge of the yard.

"What is it, boy?" she asked.

Biscuit barked and wagged his tail. He buried his nose back into the leaves. Emily pushed the dog aside and brushed some of the leaves out of the way. Tucked in a shallow spot in the yard was a brown box turtle with splotches of bright yellow.

"Sam! Come here!" she yelled. "I think Biscuit found Chomper!"

Sam ran over. He looked down and grinned when he saw the turtle. "It is Chomper!" he squealed. "I recognize that yellow patch by his right leg. But how did he get here?"

"I don't know, but let's get him back in his

pen," Emily said. "Can you take Biscuit back in the house?"

While Sam grabbed the dog by his collar and pulled him into the house, Emily carefully lifted the turtle and took him to his enclosure.

"I brought him some food," Sam said as he returned from the house. He placed a handful of fresh lettuce onto the tray. Chomper immediately headed for his feeding spot and took a big crunchy bite.

"He looks happy to be back in his home," Emily said. "See, Chomper, you've got everything you need here. Food, water, sunlight, and, most importantly, a safe place away from pesky dogs."

"Yeah, what more could you ask for?" Sam asked.

Chomper turned his head and looked at Sam and Emily.

"It's almost like he's listening to us," Emily said happily.

Chomper took another bite of lettuce and then slowly turned. He plodded over to the pen gate.

"Where are you going, buddy?" Sam asked. "The gate's locked."

Chomper took another look at the twins

and then extended his neck and pushed the hook out of the way with his head. Another push had the gate swinging open on its hinges.

"Did you see that?" Sam asked in amazement.

"Are you kidding me?" Emily asked. "It looks like no one let Chomper out of his pen after all. He did it all by himself."

They watched as the turtle slowly walked through the pen gate. He turned and started walking toward the far edge of the yard. His pace was slow but steady.

"Where do you think he's going?" Emily asked.

"It looks like he's headed back toward that pile of leaves."

"But why would he leave?" Emily asked sadly. "We fed him and gave him water."

"And built him this beautiful pen," Sam added.

"Well, I'm going to get him," Emily said. "Maybe we can move the hook to the outside so he can't open it."

"I don't know, Emily."

"You don't know what?"

"I don't know if we should keep him in the pen if he really doesn't want to be there," Sam said.

"But why wouldn't he?" she persisted. "That doesn't make any sense."

"I don't know, maybe it does," Sam said thoughtfully. "I mean, Chomper is a wild animal after all. I guess he just prefers to be free."

"Hmm. Maybe you're right," his sister said. Chomper had almost reached the leaves.

"We should take him to the park, so he'll be safe from Biscuit," Sam said.

"But what about other animals?" Emily asked.

"I guess we have to hope his shell can protect him."

"I'm sure going to miss him."

"Yeah, me too," Sam said.

Emily looked at the pen they had built. "And what are we going to do with this pen we worked so hard on?"

Sam smiled slyly. "How about we find a nice snake to keep in it? I'm sure Mateo will help us catch one."

Emily grimaced. "Haven't I told you I hate snakes?"

Her brother grinned. "Only about a hundred times."

The End

Box Turtles

A box turtle is the common name for a breed of turtle that has a shell shaped like a dome. The shell is hinged at the bottom to allow the turtle to close its shell. This allows the turtle to escape enemies who can't get through its hard shell. Box turtles are popular pets, but you should talk to your parents about how to care for them because they can become stressed if you touch them too much. They can also be injured by dogs, cats, and neighborhood animals. Pet box turtles should live in an enclosed outdoor location with lots of sunlight.

Box turtles are friendly! They are often found hanging out together and sometimes even share a hibernation spot in the winter.

In the wild, they eat insects, berries, worms, roots, flowers, and small animals such as fish, frogs, snakes, and even birds. At the zoo, they are fed salad, earthworms, and crickets. Box turtles can live for a long time, sometimes over one hundred years!

Garter Snakes

Like box turtles, garter snakes are reptiles. They are cold-blooded, which means they often lay out in the sun to warm their bodies. Garter snakes can be found in yards, gardens, and forests, usually in areas near water.

Garter snakes are carnivores! They will eat earthworms, snails, insects like grasshoppers, fish and sometimes even rodents like mice and small birds. They swallow their prey whole. If they can overpower it, they'll eat it!

Like box turtles, garter snakes are friendly. They sometimes hibernate in the winter with hundreds of other snakes.

Garter snakes move by wiggling their bodies in an S-shape. They can also swim and even climb trees, so you never know where you're going to see one.

And here's one more fact about garter snakes that Emily would hate: females give birth to 15–40 snakes at one time! That's a lot of snakes!

Where Did Sam and Emily's Last Name Come From?

I chose Sam and Emily's last name after David Hilbert, who is a famous mathematician. In 1900, he proposed twenty-three math problems across many areas of mathematics, many of which are still unsolved to this day.

For Teachers and Parents

While I hope *The Case of the Missing Turtle* and other **Emily** and **Sam** books are entertaining to read, they also contain some important concepts from the Common Core curriculum.

Here are some of the first grade Common Core math lessons represented in this book:

- Measure lengths indirectly and by iterating length units.
  - o **1.MD.A.2** Express the length of an object as a whole number of length units, by laying multiple copies of a shorter object (the length unit) end to end; understand that the length measurement of an object is the

number of same-size length units that span it with no gaps or overlaps.

- Represent and interpret data.
  - o **1.MD.C.4** Organize, represent, and interpret data with up to three categories; ask and answer questions about the total number of data points, how many in each category, and how many more or less are in one category than in another.

- Reason with shapes and their attributes.
  - o **1.G.A.1** Distinguish between defining attributes (e.g., triangles are closed and three-sided) versus non-defining attributes (e.g., color, orientation, overall size); build and draw shapes to possess defining attributes.
  - o **1.G.A.2** Compose two-dimensional shapes (rectangles, squares, trapezoids, triangles, half-circles, and quarter-circles) or three-dimensional shapes (cubes, right rectangular prisms, right circular cones, and right circular cylinders) to create a composite shape.

The Mad Scientist Next Door

A Science Adventure

Book 2
in the **Emily and Sam** Series
by
Dave Cole

The New Neighbor

Sam Hilbert and his twin sister Emily waved goodbye to their friend Affan and his mother, who had dropped them off at their house following soccer practice. They were headed to their house when they saw the moving van parked in front of the house next door. The house had been empty all summer and they had been wondering if it was going to stay that way forever.

"It looks like someone is finally moving in," Sam said as he examined the large yellow truck.

"I hope they have kids our age," Emily said.

"I hope it's a boy," her brother replied.

"A girl."

"No, a boy," Sam insisted.

"What about one of each?" his sister asked.

He thought about it for a moment. "Yeah, that would work."

The front door of the house was open, and the twins watched as the movers used a lift on the truck to lower a couch to the ground. The two muscular men then carried it into the house.

"See any bikes or toys or anything?" Sam asked as he peered into the back of the truck.

"Not yet," Emily answered. "Just furniture and boxes."

"Could be boxes of toys," Sam reasoned.

"Could be."

The two movers nodded a greeting to the kids as they returned from the house. Sam and Emily watched as the men carried in a bed frame, four chairs, and a dining room table. There was still no sign of anything that looked like it belonged to a kid.

"It's not looking good," Emily said.

"Nope."

"Maybe they've already moved in the kid stuff," Emily said hopefully. "The truck is half empty."

"Maybe," Sam said. "Or maybe there's another truck coming."

"I still haven't seen our new neighbors," Emily said.

The words were barely out of her mouth when a small blue car pulled up to the curb and backed in to a spot in front of the moving van.

Emily and Sam looked on eagerly. Emily crossed her fingers on both hands. If the new neighbor had kids, they would be getting out of the car any time now.

"Any sign of kids?" she asked.

"Not yet."

The car door slammed shut with a loud thunk. The twins listened for the sound of running feet but there was just the clomp of adult footsteps. They waited for the person to come around the front of the moving van. What they saw next was completely unexpected.

It was a man with white hair that stood out everywhere in thick clumps. He had huge round glasses with thick lenses secured to his head with a navy blue band. He was wearing a pair of bright-green pants tucked into canvas boots that looked too big for his feet. What stood out the most, though, was the white lab coat that went almost all the way down to his boots.

"Do you think he's a scientist or something?" Emily asked.

"Either that or a circus clown," Sam answered.

They watched in silence as the strange man walked to the back of the truck. The two moving men were lowering a large crate.

"Be very careful with that," their new neighbor said.

"What's in here?" asked one of the movers.

"Whatever it is, it sure is heavy," said the other.

"Your job is to move it, not ask questions," the man in the lab coat barked.

"Fine. Where do you want it?"

"In the garage. And be careful!"

The man used a remote control to open the garage door. When the door had rolled up, Emily and Sam could see inside. One entire wall of the garage was lined with large tables covered in boxes, some marked with danger symbols. As the twins watched, their new neighbor carefully removed a microscope from one of the boxes.

"Wow! Look at all that stuff," Sam said.

"He's got a whole lab in there!" Emily gasped.

The movers lowered the crate onto the concrete floor of the garage.

"Do you want us to help you get the crate open?" one asked. "I've got a crowbar in the truck."

"No! No one but me touches what's inside," the man in the lab coat said sharply. "That should be it for the garage. Everything else goes in the house."

As soon as the movers left the garage, the man pushed the button on the remote and the door began to slide down. As it did, the man finally noticed Emily and Sam and fixed his eyes on them with a frown. Then the door closed and he was lost to sight.

"What do you think is in that crate?" Sam asked.

"No clue," Emily said. "I just know our new neighbor doesn't seem very friendly."

"Mad scientists usually aren't," Sam said in a voice filled with concern.

Acknowledgments

Thanks to the amazing team at Common Deer Press: Kirsten Marion for seeing the vision of this new series, Erin Della Mattia for her great editing work, and Emily Stewart for those important final touches (and for giving me a great character name). Thanks to Matty Mitchell for the beautiful illustrations that perfectly capture Emily and Sam throughout their adventures.

Thanks to my family for always being there for me. Stephanie, Jordan, and Justin are the best kids a dad could hope for and Debbie is the kind of wife who gives me the time and space to let me work on books even when we're on vacation.

And a special thanks to all the readers of the Emily and Sam and The Math Kids series. I always love to hear from you. If you want to contact me or keep up with what's going on with Emily and Sam and the Math Kids, you can visit www.theMathKids.com.